This book belongs to

_____

To my awesome black son,
I want you to
always know that
You are my JOY,
my PRIDE, and
my LOVE!

Written by Ugo Arthur Ezeoke
Character Illustrations by Miracle Ndubueze - @mr_m.art
Designed by Christiana Unaeze

Printed in the United States of America

First Printing, 2020

This book is dedicated to you,
my handsome black son.

Always remember that
no matter what anyone else says or thinks,
you truly are amazing, handsome, and awesome!

I want you to
be happy, always!

This is why
I take you to the park ...

... just so i can
watch you play,
have fun,

and run around happily!

You make me
very happy and proud
when you help me cook
and do chores
around the house.

I want to see you grow
and become more and more
handsome and awesome!

... So i do my best
to make the
"yummiest" dishes
for you!

Watching your eyes light up as you open the presents I buy for you, simply feels like MAGIC!

I feel So proud and blessed when you hug me and Say, "thank you for my presents mummy."

I love to spend time with you, watching you as you play with your toys, or singing your favorite songs together!

My handsome son,
I just want you to know
that I will always love you!

But God loves you even more!

So, you must always thank God
for the many blessings
you enjoy.

Always pray and ask God
to bless our family,
and bless our loved ones,
and bless the sick and the poor.

Amen.

I enjoy reading your favorite bedtime stories to you!

And when
story time is over,
and it is time
to tuck you into bed,
I want you to
always remember these

three important truths:

1: You are HANDSOME!

2: You are AWESOME!

3: I love you forever
and ever, and EVER!

Now it's time to
close your eyes my son;
Sleep and dream beautiful
dreams.

Tomorrow, you will wake up,
brighter and more handsome
than ever before,
to light up my life
all over again!

God bless you
my awesome black son.
I will always love you!

Love, Mommy.

My Awesome Black Son

written by Ugo Arthur Ezeoke

character illustrations by
Miracle Ndubueze

designed by
Christiana Unaeze

Made in the USA
Middletown, DE
04 April 2022